A Memory-Filled Antique

THE ROCKING CHAIR

Jeanette Foster

ISBN 978-1546994923

ArtsyAvenue.com

To my husband, Parker, who is very much like this precious rocking chair. Our settings change and time passes but just as this rocking chair is a place of rest, a familiar comfort, and a source of joy so is his presence to my heart.

And for my Heavenly Father's glory.

A creaky rocking chair,
What stories she could tell!
Her wood and seat have been well loved
Her owner she served well.

Began she as a cradle,
An infant in her laid,
For many quiet hours she rocked,
Sweet memories were made.

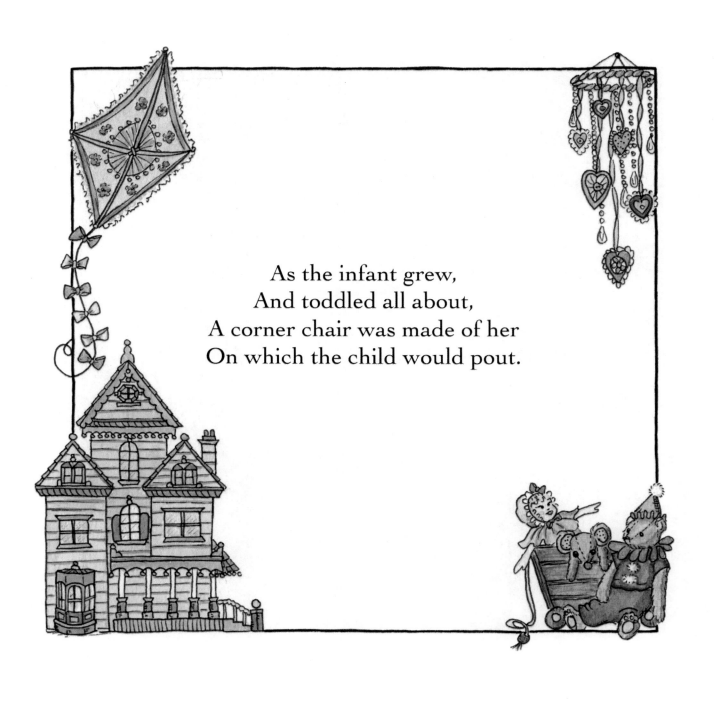

As the infant grew,
And toddled all about,
A corner chair was made of her
On which the child would pout.

The child grew too tall
To sit upon the chair,
So Papa made it bigger,
Upholstry she did wear.

Extra comfort added,
A tiny floral print,
With feathers she was padded,
Brass buttons that did glint.

She was there for tea,
Piano practice too,
Entertaining giggling friends,
Helped to tie a shoe.

So many special things
Upon her frame was sat,
Hats and gloves and purses,
Quilts, letters, books, and cats!

One eventful day
A stranger on her set,
With cuff, collar, and calonge,
A hopeful, honest gent.

His visits become often,
The chair became his place,
Until the day he left it,
On his knee...opened a case!

Excitement in the house!
A dress, a ring, a veil!
The date and decorations
All planned with much detail.

Moved to a new home,
Much change did then occur,
A pair of wooden rockers
Were nailed onto her.

Many hours of sewing,
Nights of knitting work,
Shelling peas and greenbeans,
Sipping coffee freshly perked.

Nights of endless rocking,
Infants crys were heard,
Years of tots and kiddies,
Sleeping cats that purred.

Often settings changed,
Her occupant did too -
Mother, Grandpa, caller,
Kitchen, hearth, bedroom.

Everything gets older,
Her wood began to creak,
Slow and steady she became
A memory-filled antique.

Finally she rested
Upon a country porch.
A pillow and an afgahn
Were added for comfort.

The child now a lady,
A lady filled with years,
Upon the rocking chair did rest
That rocker now so dear.

The rocker gives a lesson -
Be always steady, true,
Continue serving everyone,
Let others be your view.

Years and years from now
Her value only grows.
A valuable collectable
With selfless service glows.

...whosoever of you will be the
chiefest, shall be **servant** of all.
For even the Son of man
came not to be ministered unto,
but to minister, and to give his life
a ransom for many.

Mark 10:44,45

Jeanette's Biography

Jeanette discovered her love for art as a child growing up in southern Wisconsin. Her home education gave her the unique opportunity to cultivate her artistic interests, which began with pencil drawings and short poems.

At age seventeen, Jeanette's family moved to rural southwest Missouri where she further developed her art style and love for poetry.

In her college years she enjoyed studying English and American literature. As the years passed, Jeanette continued to compose numerous stories in the style she grew to love best - rhyme. After getting married, Jeanette's husband encouraged her to bring her stories to life with illustrations. She was confident watercolor was the classic medium which would give her stories the flavor she wanted. She invested hours of study to teach herself the art of watercolor.

Jeanette's vision is to provide colorful, fun, family-friendly stories that everyone can enjoy over and over. She writes and illustrates her books to shine the love and truth of Jesus, while coaxing giggles from both young and old. Jeanette loves her Lord and Savior, Jesus Christ, and lives happily with her husband who works closely with her to bring every story to life. Together they dream, write, and edit each classic tale their publishing company delivers to you. You can stay up to date on Jeanette's latest works and read her blog at ArtsyAvenue.com.